Rhymes for Two Voices

FARMER'S DOG

Goes to the Forest

By
David L. Harrison

Illustrated by
Arden Johnson-Petrov

Wordsong
Boyds Mills Press

Published by Wordsong
Boyds Mills Press, Inc.
A Highlights Company
815 Church Street
Honesdale, Pennsylvania 18431
Printed in China

Harrison, David L.
   Farmer's dog in the forest : more rhymes for two voices / by David L.
Harrison ; illustrated by Arden Johnson-Petrov.— 1st ed.
      p. cm.
   ISBN 1-59078-242-9 (alk. paper)
   1. Dogs—Juvenile poetry. 2. Forests and forestry—Juvenile poetry.
3. Children's poetry, American. I. Johnson-Petrov, Arden. II. Title.
   PS3608.A7834F37 2005
   811'.6—dc22
         2004028851

First edition, 2005
The text of this book is set in 18-point Janson Text and Janson Text Italic.
The illustrations are done in pastel.

Visit our Web site at www.boydsmillspress.com

10 9 8 7 6 5 4 3 2 1

With love to Alexis Marie, our next reader
—D. L. H.

To Mike, the master artist
—A. P.

Trail

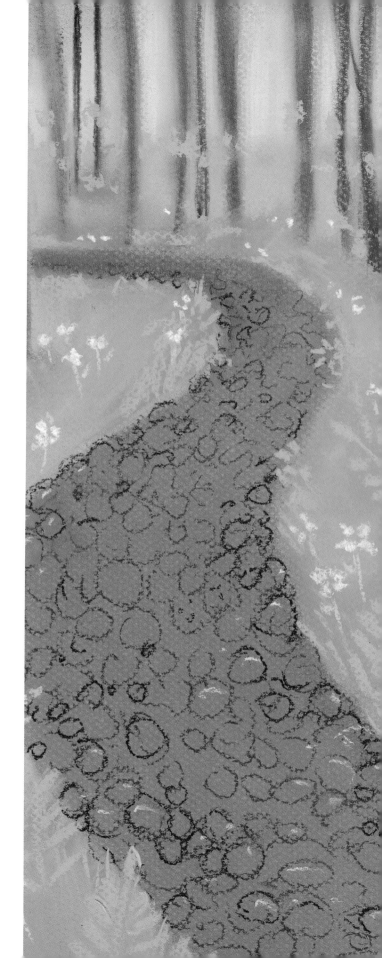

Trail, Trail,
what do you see?

*The forest waiting
for you and me!*

Trail, Trail,
how will you go?

*Wandering slowly
to and fro.*

Trail, Trail,
can I come, too?

*We'll have fun!
I promise you!*

Tortoise

Tortoise, Tortoise,
why so slow?

I have no place
I need to go.

Don't you ever
want to roam?

Wherever I am
I'm always home.

Caterpillar

Caterpillar, Caterpillar,
you look mean!

*I'm very hairy,
scary, green!*

Who do you want
to scare away?

*Birds! They hunt me
every day!*

The fatter you get,
the harder they'll try!

*I'll trick them
as a butterfly!*

Spider

Spider, Spider,
looking thinner.

*Haven't had
a thing for dinner!*

Maybe you built
your web too high.

*I want to catch
a buzzy fly!*

And if the fly
just buzzes by?

*I'll sit here by myself
and sigh.*

Woodpecker

Woodpecker,
Woodpecker,
what do you see?

*Juicy bugs
inside this tree!*

How do you find them
in the dark?

*I rat-a-tat-tat
right through the bark.*

Tree

Tree, Tree,
You're so tall!

I'm the mightiest
plant of all.

What do you do
when weather is dry?

Find some water
so I won't die.

What do you use
to get a drink?

My roots run deeper
than you think!

Crow

Crow, Crow,
why so proud?

> *My eyes are sharp,*
> *my voice is loud.*

Why do you choose
the tallest tree?

> *I sit up high*
> *where I can see.*

What if danger
lurks below?

> *I caw my friends*
> *and off we go!*

Squirrel

Squirrel, Squirrel,
what's the matter?

*I'm so mad
it makes me chatter!*

Why are you chattering
in a tree?

*That nosy fox
was sniffing me!*

After he leaves,
what will you do?

*Maybe I'll eat
a nut or two.*

Tree Frog

Tree Frog, Tree Frog,
how's your day?

> *I'm under a leaf,*
> *dozing away.*

What do you plan
to do tonight?

> *Sing my song*
> *with all my might!*

Owl

Owl, Owl,
why do you think
you're looking sort of grumpy?

*Last night I never
slept a wink,
which makes me very grumpy!*

Last night if you
had gone to bed,
you wouldn't be so grumpy.

*I'd like to sleep
today instead.
So, you are making me
grumpy!*

Moth

Moth, Moth,
why so quiet?

Don't want to be
on someone's diet!

Why do you sit
so still that way?

Shhh! I'm hiding!
Go away!

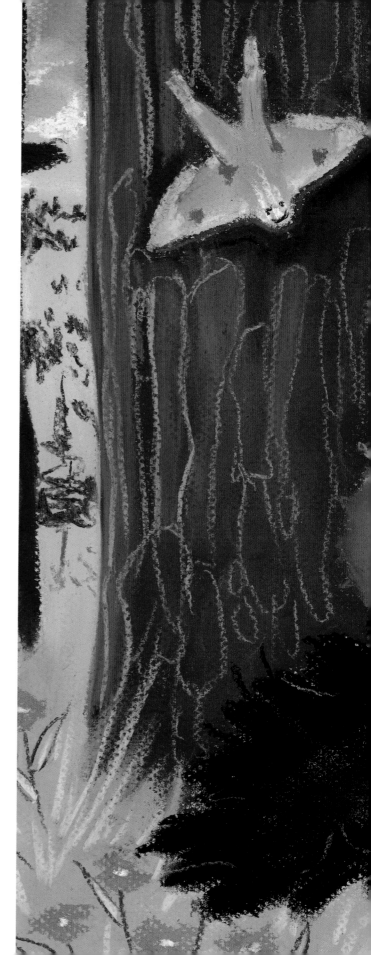

Brook

Brook, Brook,
where do you flow?

Between my banks
wherever they go.

I could jump across,
I bet.

If you miss,
you'll get all wet!

Like those fishes
in your pool?

Come on in,
my water's cool.

Grass

Grass, Grass,
thick and sweet,
deep, deep in the forest.

We love to offer
deer a treat
deep, deep in the forest.

What do you do
when cold winds blow
deep, deep in the forest?

Wait for spring
to melt the snow
deep, deep in the forest.

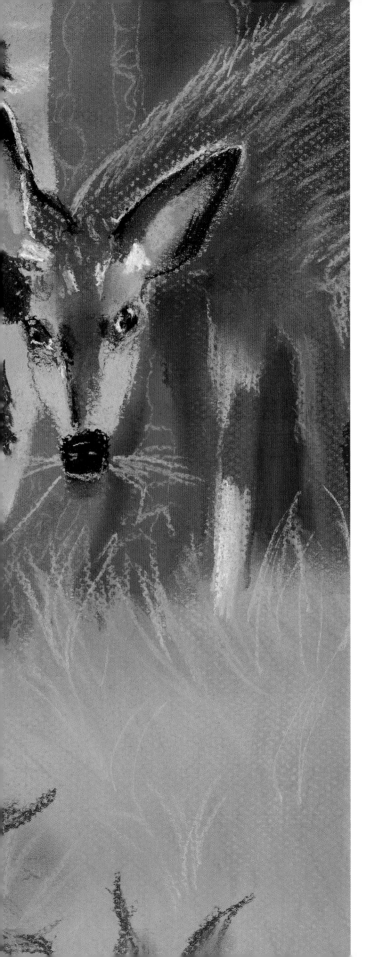

Doe

Doe, Doe,
gentle deer,
do you like the forest?

Yes, I do!
I love it here.
My home is in the forest.

What do you find
that's good to eat,
living in the forest?

Yummy grass,
thick and sweet.
Mmm! I love the forest!

Farmer

Farmer, Farmer,
what do you see
in the field beside the forest?

*My good old dog
is back with me
in the field beside the forest.*